Princess Katie's Kittens

Princess Katie's Kittens

Suki in the Snow

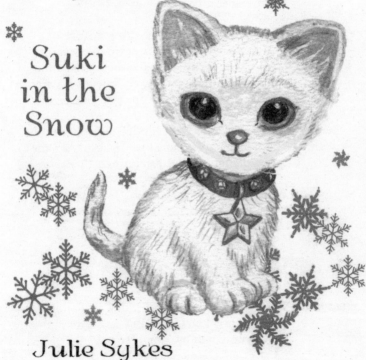

Julie Sykes

PICCADILLY PRESS · LONDON

For Roger, Emma,
Charlie and Will

First published in Great Britain in 2012
by Piccadilly Press Ltd,
5 Castle Road, London NW1 8PR
www.piccadillypress.co.uk

A catalogue record for this book is available
from the British Library

ISBN: 978 1 84812 258 1 (paperback)

1 3 5 7 9 10 8 6 4 2

Printed in the UK by CPI Group (UK) Ltd, Croydon, CR0 4YY
Croydon, CR1 4PD
Cover design by Simon Davis
Cover illustration by Sue Hellard

Chapter 1

Going on Holiday

'Look!' cried Princess Katie of Tula, staring out of her bedroom window. 'The helicopter's here.'

Becky Philips raced to the window, just in time to see the royal helicopter landing on the lawn.

'We'd better hurry,' said Katie, grabbing

her pink rucksack. 'We've still got to take the kittens down to the stables.'

It was the spring holidays and Princess Katie and her family were going on a skiing trip to the mountains in the north of Tula. Even better, this year Katie's best friend Becky and Becky's mum, the royal house-keeper, were coming with them! Miss Blaze, Katie's riding teacher, was going to look after all of Katie's kittens while she was on holiday.

'I wish we didn't have to leave the kittens behind. I'm going to miss them a lot,' said Katie.

'Me too,' Becky agreed. 'I wonder what they'd think of snow,' said Katie, pulling on her boots with the cosy fur lining.

'They'd hate it. They'd get cold paws,' giggled Becky.

Katie and Becky ran downstairs to the boot room and found Alfie giving Bella a cuddle.

'Did you come to say goodbye too?' he asked.

'Yes,' said Katie, putting her rucksack down and walking over to the basket where the other five kittens were curled up together. Katie and Becky stroked each of them in turn.

'Bye, kittens. Be good while we're away,' said Katie

'Where's Suki going?'

Suki, the white kitten with the bright

blue eyes, suddenly jumped out of the basket, stretched her paws, then marched over to Katie's rucksack. She sniffed it curiously and stuck her head inside.

'Oh no you don't!' said Katie, giggling as she gently pulled her out. 'You wouldn't like it in there.'

Katie rummaged in her bag and pulled out her camera.

'Photo time,' she said.

Becky scooped Suki up and put her back in the basket with her brothers and sisters. Suki mewed crossly. So did Bella when Alfie put her on the floor.

'It's only for a minute, so I can take your picture,' said Katie. 'Sit still, everyone.'

'Did you get one?' asked Becky, as Suki jumped out of the basket.

'Get one what?' asked Mrs Philips, Becky's mum, coming into the room.

'A photo of the kittens,' said Katie. 'I got two, but the second one only has Suki's tail in it.'

Mrs Philips laughed. 'You'd better hurry up if you're taking the kittens to the stables. The queen asked me to tell you that the suitcases have been loaded and the helicopter is ready to leave.'

'Already?' squeaked Katie. Her stomach fluttered with excitement.

'I'll carry Bella,' said Alfie.

Six kittens were a lot to look after and Katie had given Bella to Alfie because he was so good with her. Putting Suki back in the basket, Katie gathered up her things. Then she and Becky carried the basket down to the stables. It was heavy and Suki kept trying to climb out.

'Please sit still,' said Katie, anxiously. 'Dad will be cross if I'm late. Princesses are never late.'

They arrived at the stables at the same time as the farrier who'd come to put new shoes on some of the horses.

'Leave the kittens in the barn and I'll check on them later,' said Miss Blaze, sounding distracted. 'Hurry, Princess. The king just called to ask where you were. He wants to leave right away.'

Katie and Becky put the basket in the opposite corner to the barn doors. At once the kittens jumped out and began to explore.

'Cat bowls!' said Becky, suddenly. 'We forgot to bring some down with us.'

'Bother,' said Katie. 'We'll have to go back. Alfie, go and tell Dad we won't be long.'

'OK,' said Alfie, giving Bella one last stroke before he went.

'Race you back to the palace,' Katie said to Becky, breaking into a run.

By the time they got back to the stables with the cat bowls, Katie was completely out of breath.

'Omph! This feels heavy,' she said, lifting up her rucksack and swinging it on to her shoulder.

Miss Blaze was still

busy with the farrier, so
Katie couldn't give her
any last-minute
instructions.

'I hope the kittens will be all right,' she
said, uncertainly.

'They'll be fine,' said Becky, pushing the
barn door to check it had shut properly.
'With Miss Blaze in charge, what could go
wrong?'

Suki was most indignant. Usually Katie
spent time playing with the kittens and
feeding them cat treats.
Today she'd moved their
bed to the barn and left.
But maybe she was coming

back – her bag was by the door. Suki strolled over to it.

The rucksack had an interesting smell that made her whiskers twitch. She gave it a pat. It was soft and squishy with lots of straps that jingled. Suki pounced  on a strap, flicking it and making it wiggle like a snake. She patted it again. The strap fell on her back. Spinning round, Suki batted it away. It was such fun. Suki played with the strap for ages.

When she'd had enough of that game, she walked round the bag. It had an interesting pocket on the front. She tried opening it but the pocket was tightly fastened with a metal thing. Suki didn't like the feel of the metal. It made her shudder. Careful not to touch it with her other paws, she climbed further up the bag. It was very wobbly. Slowly, using her tail to balance, she walked along the rucksack until she reached the opening at the top. Sticking her head inside, she waited for her eyes to adjust to the dimness.

The bag was crammed with lots of very interesting things. Full of curiosity, Suki stuck a paw inside and fished around. Then suddenly she was falling. She tried to save herself but there was nothing to cling on to. Stretching out her paws, Suki braced herself, but luckily a nice soft landing was waiting for her. She sat up quickly and found she was staring at a pair of glassy eyes.

'Meow!'

What was that? It was clearly an animal but it wasn't a cat or a dog. It had rounded ears and and a black nose. Fluffing out her fur to make herself look bigger, Suki hissed at it. The animal stared back without even blinking. Suki hissed again.

Nothing happened!

Cautiously she leant forward and sniffed its nose. It wasn't real! Whiskers twitching, Suki prodded the animal's arms and then its tummy. It was lovely and soft and even nicer than the cushion in her cat basket. Happily, Suki kneaded it with her paws. She would have a little rest before she explored the rest of the bag.

Neatly curling her tail around her fluffy white body, Suki closed her eyes. She was just drifting off to sleep when a loud zipping noise startled her. Suki leapt up but now it was too dark to see anything. She felt the bag rise in the air and she slid sideways. Unsheathing her claws, she sunk them into the toy animal to stop herself from sliding around. The bag bounced uncomfortably.

'Meow!'

Suki could hear voices. She recognised Katie's and thought it sounded high and excited. Suki mewed again but her cry was drowned out by laughter. The bag bounced faster as if Katie had sped up. Suki clung on and hoped that, wherever she was being taken, she'd get there soon.

Chapter 2

A Stowaway

Katie and Becky ran through the palace gardens to a flat lawn where a huge red helicopter decorated with the royal crest was waiting.

'I'll take that for you,' said Mrs Philips, reaching for Katie's rucksack. 'Goodness, this is heavy. Whatever have you got in there?'

Katie blushed.
'Not much,
a few books,
some sweets,
a camera,
my spare tiara,
Cuddles my teddy
bear and a dvd.'

The king and queen were already aboard and belted into their large comfy seats.

'Here you are at last,' said the queen, sounding relieved.

Katie sat opposite her mum and dad, choosing the seat by the window, and Becky went in the middle with Alfie next to her. Mrs Philips sat behind them with the king's butler. Once everyone was buckled in, the pilot turned on the engine and the helicopter roared to life.

Katie couldn't wait to leave and it seemed ages before the helicopter's rotor blades had warmed up enough to take off. But at last they were rising smoothly into the air and Starlight Towers was shrinking away beneath them.

Katie kept her nose pressed to the window until a high-pitched squeak made her jump. She turned around quickly, but everyone, even the queen who wasn't keen on flying, was looking out of the windows. Maybe it had just been Katie's seat – leather often made funny squeaky noises.

Katie forgot about it as she was caught up in the excitement of watching the doll-sized houses, the miniature roads and tiny fields passing beneath them. She loved it best of all

when they flew up through swirling white clouds.

After a while, Katie grew impatient with

flying and couldn't wait to arrive at the Tulan Alps. Suddenly she heard another squeak.

'What was that?' she said.

'What was what?' asked Becky, her eyes glued to the window.

'I heard a squeaking noise,' Katie replied.

Becky tipped her head to one side to listen. 'All I can hear is the helicopter buzzing.'

'You probably heard something on the television,' said Alfie, who was flicking through the TV channels with the remote control. 'It's all boring daytime chat shows. Some of the people on them do lots of squeaking. Can we watch your dvd, Katie?'

'OK,' said Katie, thinking it would

be a good way to pass the time.

She unzipped her rucksack and put her hand inside.

'Eeek!' she squealed, quickly pulling it back again. Her green eyes widened. 'There's something soft and fluffy in my rucksack!'

'That's just Cuddles,' said Becky with a giggle.

'But it moved!' said Katie. Cautiously, she opened her rucksack up wider. Then she gasped.

'Oh no! You're not going to believe this.'

Becky leant closer. 'Believe what?'

Katie reached into her bag and lifted out a little white kitten. 'It's Suki!' she groaned.

Looking very pleased with herself, Suki gazed round at everyone with her bright blue eyes.

'That's not fair!' said Alfie hotly. 'If I'd have known you were bringing Suki then I'd have brought Bella.'

'Katie? You've brought a kitten with you? That was *very* naughty,' said the king sternly.

'But I didn't bring her,' said Katie indignantly. 'She must have stowed away in my bag.'

The king sighed. 'Those kittens, they're nothing but trouble! How on earth are you going to look after her properly? What if she tries to find her way home? Cats don't like being moved to new places.'

Katie flushed. 'I'm sorry, Dad. I didn't mean to bring Suki, but now she's here I'll make sure she's not any trouble.'

Katie didn't like upsetting her dad but secretly she was thrilled to have Suki with her. A kitten on holiday – what fun! She glanced across at Becky and gave her a little grin. Becky grinned back.

'I'll help you,' she whispered.

'Thanks,' said Katie gratefully.

Suki wanted to go exploring, but Katie sat her in her lap and stroked her until she settled down. Purring ecstatically, Suki rubbed

her head against Katie's hand, encouraging her to scratch her behind the ears and under her chin where she liked it best.

'What about the dvd?' asked Alfie.

'Oh, sorry! It's here.' Katie handed it over.

The flight lasted for three long hours but Katie didn't mind. It was such fun having Suki with her. When Mrs Philips served a picnic lunch, Katie finally put her on the floor. It made everyone laugh to see Suki wobbling around the vibrating cabin.

At last, Katie saw the snow-covered

mountains on the horizon. Her stomach fluttered excitedly. Not long now and they'd be up there skiing!

Snatching an indignant Suki up in her arms, she buckled herself back into her seat. It was a very smooth landing, but Suki hated sitting still while the pilot waited for the helicopter's rotor blades to stop whirring. She wriggled impatiently and tried to climb from Katie's lap.

'Steady there,' soothed Katie. She couldn't wait to leave the helicopter either.

At last the helicopter doors opened and a blast of cold air rushed into the cabin.

'Coats on,' said Mrs Philips, handing them out.

'I love your new ski jacket,' said Becky enviously as Katie zipped up her pink and purple jacket.

'Thanks! I wanted the white one with the

fur hood but mum wouldn't let me in case I got lost in the snow! Yours is nice too – blue suits you.'

'In that case, Suki needs a coloured jacket too,' said Becky. 'We'll never find her if she goes outside.'

Princess Katie gulped. 'I hadn't thought of that. But Suki won't be going outside. If Dad's right and cats don't like being away from home, then I don't want her trying to find her way back to the palace. She'd definitely get lost.'

It was a shock stepping out of the warm helicopter into the cold. The frozen air made Katie's face sting. She was glad of her warm coat and thick gloves.

'Careful, Princess, the ground is icy,' said Mrs Philips, holding out a hand to help Katie down the steps.

Katie gripped Mrs Philips tightly with one hand and Suki with the other. The kitten didn't want to be carried and struggled to get free.

'It's brilliant here. Look at all the snow!' Alfie exclaimed.

'Not right now,' said Katie, gritting her teeth. Suki was wriggling like a snake and it was hard holding on to her. The royal car, a long black limousine, was waiting close by and Katie made

her way over until there was one more step to go. As Katie put her foot on the ground, she slipped on the ice. Panic flooded through her, making her feel hot and cold at the same time.

'It's all right, I've got you,' said Mrs Philips.

'Thanks,' said Katie, clutching Suki even more tightly.

They finally reached the royal limousine and the chauffeur opened the car door, but, just as Katie was about to climb in, disaster struck! Suki twisted free. She landed on all fours and, with a startled meow, she slid across the icy ground and under the stationary car.

Chapter 3

Not Again!

'Quick!' shouted Katie, crouching down. 'Catch her before she runs away!'

Becky and Alfie went around to the other side of the car to block Suki's escape, but the ice made it difficult to move quickly.

'Here, Suki!' called Katie.

She rubbed her finger and thumb

together to get Suki's attention.

Suki hesitated but kept walking. Then she noticed Becky and Alfie and hurriedly changed direction towards the boot of the car. Feet slipping on the icy ground, Katie raced after her.

'Suki,' she pleaded, 'come out of there!

Here, puss, before you freeze your paws.'

Suki thought it a great game. Changing direction again, she trotted towards the front of the car. In desperation, Katie threw herself on the ground to crawl after her.

'Stop! Princess Katie, get up at once,' said the queen.

'Sorry, Mum,' said Katie. 'But how else can I catch Suki?'

'Not like that. It's far too dangerous,' said the queen anxiously. 'What if the chauffeur didn't realise you were there and drove away? If you leave Suki alone she'll soon get bored and come out.'

It didn't sound like much of a plan, but Katie didn't have a better idea.

'Stay very still,' she told Becky and Alfie. 'But be ready to catch Suki if she moves.'

'Excuse me,' said the king, stepping forward. 'I'm not standing out here freezing while you play games with a kitten. We're leaving in two minutes.'

Katie's stomach flip-flopped. Two minutes! Would they catch Suki in such a short time? She stood very still, willing the kitten to come out in the open. Several long seconds later, her patience was rewarded. Suki crept from under the car. Katie longed to snatch her up but she forced herself to stay still. Suki walked over and nudged her nose against her Katie's leg.

'Meow,' she said.

Katie's heart was racing but she calmly bent down and stroked Suki's soft fur. The kitten purred with pleasure and nudged Katie again. Clasping her round the middle, Katie scooped her up.

'Got you!' she said.

'Hooray!' cheered Becky.

'Into the car everyone,' said the queen. 'Quickly, please.'

Katie usually loved the drive to the royal chalet but at first she was too wound up to enjoy it properly. All she could think about was Suki and the kitten things she'd need

once they arrived at the chalet.

'Cat food, bowls, a bed and a litter tray,' she mumbled. The litter tray was very important. There was no way Katie was letting Suki go outside in the snow on her own.

As they drove into the village of Blanc, the pretty ski resort at the foot of the mountains, Becky pointed out of the window.

'Look at all the flags and lights! Are they because the royal family has come to stay?'

'No,' said Katie. 'It's for the Blanc Ice Fair. It lasts all week and ends on Friday night with the Ice Extravaganza. There are lots of stalls with games and things to buy, a hog

roast, an ice-skating race and there's a competition for the best snow sculpture. The whole town turns out for it, even the children. It ends on the stroke of ten and Alfie and I are allowed to stay up for the whole thing.'

Becky's eyes shone. 'It sounds brilliant. Shall we enter the competition to build a snow sculpture?'

'Yes!' exclaimed Katie. 'Alfie and I built a snowman last year but we accidentally knocked the head off when we were putting stones on it

for eyes, so no one knew what it was.' 'It was so funny,' Alfie chuckled. 'Every entry gets a rosette and when the judges gave us ours they said well done for building a very nice mountain!'

Katie pressed her nose up against the car window. It was so exciting to be back in Blanc again. She loved the pretty wooden chalet houses with tiny lights strung from their roofs, and the way the snow made everything look like it was covered with thick white icing. She couldn't wait to get out and sledge and have snowball fights.

The royal ski chalet was on the edge of

the town. It was three storeys high, with a pointed roof and lots of chimneys. The royal flag of Tula was flying from a pole in the middle of the drive.

Katie held onto Suki very firmly as she

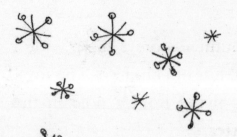

walked from the car to the huge front door, her feet crunching in the snow. Once inside, she put Suki on the wooden floor while she pulled off her snow boots. Suki stood for a moment, looking round. She stretched out her legs and with a shake of her paws set off to explore her new surroundings.

'Put her in the boot room,' said the queen. 'It'll seem most like home.'

Katie had been about to ask if she could have Suki in her bedroom,

but she knew Mum
was right. If cats
didn't like new
places, it was better
Suki kept to familiar surroundings.

The chalet boot room was much smaller
than the one in the palace and full of skis,
boots and thick coats. Suki looked round
uncertainly, her tail swishing.

'It doesn't look much now, but it'll be
just like home
when I've got
you a bed and
some toys,'
Katie told her.

'Do you
think she'll be
lonely without

her brothers and sisters?'
asked Becky.

'I expect so, but we'll
keep visiting her,' said
Katie. 'Come on, I want
to show you our bedroom
next. It's got windows that
look out two different ways, so you can see
Blanc *and* the mountains. There's just time
before our first skiing lesson.'

⭑ 🐾 ⭑

Not again! Suki
thought crossly when
Katie left her in the
boot room. She was
fed up of being shut
away. First in the

barn, then a bag, then a noisy machine that made her paws shake and her stomach tumble, and now in this room full of clumpy boots, sticks and poles. There wasn't even a bed to curl up in. Suki walked round the room twice to check she hadn't missed one.

There were no other kittens and no toys either, although the boots were fun to play with. They had thick laces that were good to pounce on. Suki teased the laces until she got her claw stuck. It took ages to get free and tugging made her paw sting. She licked it until it felt better then peered inside the boot. It was very dark and had a

strong smell that made her sneeze. Remembering how she'd been stuck inside the bag, Suki decided not to go any further.

There was a small cupboard nearby. Suki hopped on top and looked around. Could she make it to the windowsill from here? Tail twitching, she sized up the gap. The windowsill was higher than the cupboard but it wasn't that far. She fixed the windowsill with her bright blue eyes and sprang.

Eek! She'd misjudged the distance. Suki clung to the windowsill with her front paws, while her back ones and her bottom swung wildly behind her. She kicked her back legs until her paws met the wall. Pushing off hard, she boosted herself up. She landed on the windowsill nose first.

That was close.

Suki's paws twitched and her heart was thumping crazily, but at least she'd made it. She sat by the window, tail neatly curled

round her paws, looking out. Soon it began to snow. Suki gazed at the fluffy white flakes drifting down in front of her eyes. She forgot they were outside and tried to bat them, but her claws made a pinging noise on the glass.

Suddenly, she saw two girls walking in the snow. They were wrapped up with bobble

hats and huge scarves. It was only when the girls stopped and looked through the window at her that Suki realised it was Katie and Becky.

'Let me out!' she squeaked, tapping on the glass.

Tugging at Becky's arm, Katie pointed straight at her. Suki's tail twitched with excitement as both girls waved, then moved off. They were coming to get her at last! They would let her outside so she could explore. Suki jumped off the windowsill and went to wait by the door. She waited for ages but the girls didn't come.

Had they got lost? Perhaps she should go and look for them. But how was she going to get out? She stared at the door and suddenly it opened. A tall man came in, carrying a brand new cat basket. Suki ran past him and out into a hall. At one end was a door.

It was open.

Without stopping, Suki ran outside and into the snow.

Chapter 4

Suki Explores

Fat white snowflakes drifted from the sky. Suki stared at them in wonder, then she batted one experimentally. It dissolved on her paw.

That's odd.

Suki batted another snowflake and then another. At first it was fun, but after a while

her paws felt wet and icy cold. Daintily, Suki shook them dry. Then she remembered Katie and Becky.

So where are they?

The girls had to be here somewhere. Suki set off, her paws sinking into the snow. In some places it was so deep it reached her tummy. It was freezing cold, but Suki struggled on, determined to find Katie and Becky. After a while, she realised she didn't know where she was going. She stopped and sniffed at the snow for clues. It was cold and smelt watery, and it made her sneeze.

Clumps of ice began to form between her claws. She tried to shake them off but they were stuck fast. She shivered. Maybe she'd go back and wait for Katie and Becky in the warm, dry chalet. Suki turned around. The snow was coming down faster now. The sky was dark and it was hard to see.

Which way is back?

Suki searched for her old tracks, but the snow had already filled them in. With a sinking feeling, she knew she was lost.

'Meow!'
Suddenly Suki was scared.

'Look, there's Suki!' said Katie as they walked past the boot room window a few minutes before.

'Hi, Suki!' called Becky, waving.

'It's strange to see her without the other kittens,' said Katie. 'I hope she won't be lonely.'

'It's only for an hour. We'll play with her

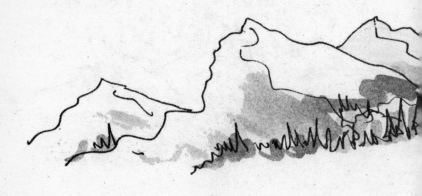

straight after our skiing lesson,' said Becky.

'OK,' said Katie, but there was a small knot of worry in her stomach that she couldn't shift.

Collecting their skis, they made their way to the foot of the mountain, where a large group of children was being sorted into two smaller groups.

'Look, there's Alfie, with my mum,' said Becky.

'He'll be in the beginner's group because this is the first time he's skied,' said Katie.

Both Katie and Becky were put in the novice group. Katie had skied twice before and Becky had taken some dry-slope skiing lessons. They lined up with the other children all dressed in thick, brightly

coloured ski trousers, coats, gloves and hats.
Mr Peak, the ski instructor, introduced
himself then went round checking that
everyone was putting their skis on correctly.

Princess Katie's feet felt strangely heavy
and she clutched her ski poles tightly to
keep her balance. Beside her, Becky looked
very nervous.

'Skiing on snow is easier than the dry
slope and much softer when you fall over,'
Katie whispered.

Becky smiled gratefully.

'Today we're skiing on the nursery slope,'
said Mr Peak. 'It's not too steep so we can
get there by the drag lift. Put your hand up
if you've never used a drag lift before.'

No one put their hand up.

'Good, let's get started then.'

It felt funny walking across the snow on skis, but Katie loved being towed uphill by the drag lift. At the top of the nursery slope, Mr Peak reminded everyone how to ski in a zigzag down the hill and how to stop by bringing the front of their skis together in a move called the snowplough. Katie's tummy

was full of butterflies while she waited for
her turn, but the moment she started skiing,
she forgot to be nervous. It was such fun
whizzing down the mountain with the cold
air rushing past her face and the snow hissing
under her skis. Reaching the bottom, she
bent her legs and turned her toes in. As the

tips of the skis came together, Katie felt herself slowing down until finally she stopped.

'Well done!' called Mr Peak.

Becky was next and her smile almost reached her ears. 'That was great fun,' she panted as she came to a wobbly halt.

For the next hour, Katie and Becky enjoyed the slow ride to the top of the

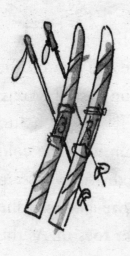

nursery slope by drag lift, and then the thrill of skiing down it. When the lesson ended, a girl with long ginger plaits started a snowball fight. Leaving their skis propped against a fence at the

bottom of the slope, Katie
and Becky joined in.

'Oomph!' yelped Katie,
as a snowball hit her in the
mouth.

She wiped the snow away before throwing
a snowball back at the boy who'd got her. It
landed on his head.

'Bullseye!' yelled Becky.

One by one, the children disappeared as
their parents came to collect them.

'Look, there's Mum,' said Becky.

'And Alfie,' said Katie, gently throwing a
snowball at her brother.

It hit him in the chest.

'Grrr!' shouted Alfie, but he was laughing
as he scooped up a handful of snow, rolled it
into a ball and threw it back.

'You missed!' called Katie, dancing around, then squealing as Alfie threw another snowball that exploded on her arm.

'Good shot, Alfie!' said Katie, smiling.

Mrs Philips watched from a safe distance until finally everyone had had enough.

'My fingers are freezing,' said Katie through chattering teeth.

'So are mine! Look how wet my gloves are,' said Becky, holding out her sodden hands.

'We'll put everything in the boiler room. Your clothes will soon dry in there,' said Mrs Philips, as they collected their skis. 'I'll make some hot chocolate when we get back to the chalet.'

'With whipped cream and marshmallows?' asked Katie.

'Definitely,' Mrs Philips agreed.

Katie's legs were aching from all the exercise but the thought of hot chocolate kept her going. She was looking forward to it so much she didn't notice the bedraggled bundle of fur crouched under a hedge as she approached the chalet gates.

'Meow,' squeaked the animal sadly.

'Look!' said Alfie pointing. 'It's a kitten.'

'Where?' asked Katie, squinting. 'Oh, I see it now. Poor thing! '

The kitten was very bedraggled. Its dirty fur stuck up in spiky clumps and it was trembling with the cold.

'We can't leave it here,' said Katie. 'We'll have to take it back to the chalet.'

Mrs Philips looked doubtful. 'I'm not sure the king will be happy about you rescuing more kittens. Maybe we should take it to the town instead?'

'But it's half frozen. It'd be quicker to take it home.'

'It looks just like Suki,' said Becky as Katie stooped to pick it up.

'It *is* Suki!' exclaimed Katie, turning hot with fright. 'How did she get out here?'

Katie hugged Suki close to her. The kitten's heart was hammering almost as fast as her own.

'I'm sorry,' she whispered. 'I was having so much fun, I forgot about you. But you mustn't go wandering off alone. It was lucky we found you. You might have got lost in the snow. I promise I'll spend more time playing with you, but you have to promise you won't wander off again.'

'Purrrip!' squeaked Suki, licking Katie on the nose.

'Good,' said Katie, swallowing back a tear. 'Come on. Let's get you home.'

Chapter 5

The Igloo

Early each morning, before Katie and Becky went skiing, they visited the boot room to play with Suki.

'She loves her new toys,' said Becky, rolling a jingly ball across the floor, and giggling as Suki skittered after it.

'I'm sure she misses her brothers and

sisters,' said Katie with a worried sigh. The days were so full with skiing, visits to the town and having fun in the snow that there wasn't much time to spend with Suki. Katie hated the way the kitten cried and tried to squeeze through the door after them every time they left her alone.

'Let's take her to visit our igloo,' said Becky. 'She'd love that.'

Katie looked uncertain. 'But what if we lose her outside?'

'We wouldn't put her down unless it was inside the igloo,' said Becky, sensibly.

Katie thought about that.

'We'd have to be very careful,' she said eventually. 'But I think Suki would like to go out, wouldn't you, puss? Right then, after our ski lesson, we'll take you to our igloo.'

The igloo was Katie and Becky's entry for the snow sculpture competition at the Ice Extravaganza. It was almost finished, with just the roof to complete.

After their skiing lesson, Mr Peak and Miss Speed, Alfie's ski instructress, organised a massive snowball fight between their two groups. Everyone was given fifteen minutes to prepare. Katie completely forgot about Suki as she threw herself into the task of rolling snowballs. When the snowball fight started, her group had an enormous pile of round white balls to throw at Alfie's group. Soon the air was thick with flying snow.

'Ooh, that's cold!' squealed Katie as a snowball exploded down the back of her neck.

'Eew! That one got me in the mouth!' Becky chuckled.

When the last snowball had been thrown, Mrs Philips, who'd been watching from a

distance, insisted that Katie, Becky and Alfie went back to the chalet for a mug of hot chocolate to warm up.

'And then we'll take Suki to see our igloo,' said Katie, guiltily remembering her promise to the kitten.

'There won't be time,' said Mrs Philips. 'You're going ice skating with your parents.'

Katie felt torn. She loved ice skating but it would mean leaving Suki alone again. For a second she wished Suki hadn't stowed away in her bag, but that made her feel even more guilty. After all, it was partly her fault. If only she hadn't left her bag lying around!

Sighing softly, Katie thought how much she loved her kittens. Being a cat owner meant caring for them all the time and not just when it was convenient. Determined to

make it up to Suki, she collected her from
the boot room to share her hot chocolate.
Suki loved whipped cream and was very
happy to lick it from Katie's finger.

'That tickles,' Katie giggled as Suki's
rough tongue lapped up the cream.

Suki didn't want to go back to the boot room by herself after that. She cried pitifully, fixing Katie with her large blue eyes as she shut the door yet again.

'I'll take you out this afternoon,' promised Katie, wishing Suki didn't look so sad.

'You go skating and I'll stay and play with Suki,' said Becky generously.

'Becky!' Katie gave her a hug. 'You're such a good friend. But that's far too generous and I can't let you. This is your holiday too. If anyone's staying home, it should be me!'

The more Katie thought about it, the more she reasoned that she should miss the ice skating and stay home with Suki. But the king wouldn't hear of it.

'Suki will be fine,' he said. 'Besides, I hardly

have any time to spend with my family. This will be the first time we've done something together in ages.'

Katie was secretly relieved that dad wanted her to go ice skating.

'I'll make it up to Suki later,' she promised herself.

The ice skating rink was on the other side of the town from the royal chalet. The king had organised an open carriage, drawn by reindeer, to take them there. It was such fun trotting along the road to the jingle of sleigh bells. The carriage driver had a pocket full of sliced-up carrots. When they arrived at the ice rink, he let Katie, Becky and Alfie feed them to the reindeer.

'Their noses feel like velvet,' said Katie, stroking the reindeer she was feeding.

'This is such a brilliant holiday,' sighed Becky happily.

'It's even better than last year, because you're here,' Katie added.

The ice rink was lit with strings of coloured fairy lights.

'It's so pretty!' said Becky.

'Wait until you see the Ice Extravaganza,' said Katie. 'It's dark then and they light the ice with different colours. They also have a DJ to play music.'

'Three more days!' said Becky. 'Do you think we'll get our igloo finished in time?'

Katie chuckled. 'Who knows, but it can't be any worse than our entry last year. At least it actually looks like an igloo!'

It was such fun swooping over the ice on skates. At first, Katie had to tow her friend, but before long Becky was so confident on the ice that she challenged the king to a race!

'Did you let me win?' she asked, when the king finished a long way behind.

'Certainly not,' he answered, winking at Katie.

Skating and being out in the fresh air gave everyone a huge appetite. They rode back to the palace on the reindeer sledge for a hearty lunch organised by Mrs Philips. It was late afternoon by the time Katie and Becky were able to slip away.

They went straight to the boot room. Suki was very happy to see the girls. Purring loudly, she wound her silky body around Katie's legs. Katie borrowed a spare scarf she'd found in the boot room, wrapped Suki in it and carried her outside. The igloo was a short walk from the chalet grounds.

'Even with a hole in the roof, it's not bad,' said Katie, walking around it.

On gloved hands and knees, she crawled through the short tunnel entrance. There was just enough room for Becky to squeeze inside with her, but there wasn't room to stand up. Making a nest for Suki with the scarf, who then curled up and slept, they went outside to work on the roof. The snow lay so thick on the ground, it was easy to shape it into snow bricks.

'One more and we're done,' said Katie, a long while later. Her breath rushed out in a cloud of steam. 'Let's put the last brick on together.'

Carefully, they lifted the brick but, as they reached over to fit it into place, Katie felt something brushing against her boot.

'Suki!' she exclaimed glancing down. Her stomach twisted in alarm. 'How long have you been there?'

'Meow!' said Suki, waving her tail.

'Becky, can you manage on your own?'

When Becky nodded, Katie let go of the brick and quickly scooped Suki up. It was disappointing to miss out on finishing the igloo, but Katie was scared that Suki might wander off again and it was very hard to see her in the snow.

'It looks fantastic,' she said, clutching Suki as she stood back to admire it.

'It's warm too,' said Becky, crawling inside.

Katie lifted Suki up so their noses were touching.

'Of all the kittens to stow away, why did it have to be you?' she said, half-crossly. 'You mustn't keep wandering off. I might never find you if you get lost in the snow!'

'Meow!' squeaked Suki, struggling to get free.

Katie sighed and put her down in the igloo tunnel.

'Go on, then,' she said, giving her a gentle pat on the bottom. 'Go and see what it's like inside the igloo, now it's finished.'

Chapter 6

🐾

The Ice Extravaganza

The following days passed in a whirl of skiing, ice skating, snowball fights and sledging on an old wooden sledge that had once belonged to the king. On the afternoon of the Ice Extravaganza, the queen made Katie, Becky and Alfie go to their rooms for a sleep.

'But I wanted to play with Suki!' said Katie.

'Suki will be fine,' said the queen firmly. 'It's going to be a late night. It would be a shame if you were too tired to enjoy it properly.'

Katie didn't think there was any chance of that. It was impossible to sleep and she and Becky lay on their beds, watching the snowflakes drift past the windows. As the afternoon passed, the sky darkened dramatically and it began to snow more heavily. A strong wind drove the snowflakes against the glass, banking them up on the window ledge.

Katie got up and peered outside. 'I hope they don't cancel the Ice Extravaganza,' she said.

'Especially after we've spent the afternoon resting,' Becky agreed. 'Do you think we can get up now?'

Katie looked at her watch. 'I should think so. It's almost time for tea. If we're quick, we could go and see Suki first.'

But as they went down the three flights of stairs, they met the queen coming up.

'I was just coming to get you,' she said. 'The Mayor of Blanc and his wife are here. Go and get Alfie, then come to the drawing room to say hello.'

Katie opened her mouth to protest. Then she remembered she was a princess and would be expected to meet the mayor, so she she shut it again quickly. As she ran back upstairs to get

Alfie, she crossed her fingers tightly and hoped the mayor and his wife wouldn't stay too long.

Suki was cross and bored. She missed her brothers and sisters and she'd not seen as much of Katie as usual either. The excitement of the new toys had soon worn off. There had been lots of visitors to the boot room but no one ever stayed long –

they snatched up boots, skis, jackets and scarves and then left. Most people didn't even speak to

Suki unless it was to tell her to, 'Go back,' as they went out. So she could hardly believe it that dark afternoon, when one of the chalet servants came in to collect a coat and rushed out without closing the door properly. Suki didn't waste a second. Following him out, she scampered away in the opposite direction.

A lovely smell was coming from a room at the end of the corridor. On silent paws, Suki padded towards it and slipped inside. Several people were rushing about. Lightly, Suki jumped on to a chair and, reaching up, rested her front paws on the table. Her blue eyes widened at the mountain of food spread out before her. All of it was covered with a clear plastic film that punctured easily with her claws but was impossible to remove.

Never mind.

Although the food smelt delicious, she wasn't really hungry and could wait until Katie fed her. Softly, Suki jumped down from the table at the same time as someone opened the outside door. Now that was tempting! Without stopping to think, Suki ran outside.

It was snowing again. Jumping and twirling, Suki batted the thick white snowflakes as they tumbled down from the sky. As she whirled and spun, she didn't realise how far she was travelling.

A long while later, Suki decided she'd had enough of the snow. It was much colder now. Her fur was stuck together in sodden clumps and balls of ice clung to the backs of her legs. She tried to shake them loose but the ice stuck fast, pulling her fur and making it sore. She was so preoccupied, she didn't notice the dog bounding towards her until it was almost too late. It was tall and

hairy, with drools of spit hanging from a long tongue. Arching her back, Suki hissed at it, then turned and fled. The dog chased after her. Seeing a bush, Suki dived under it, but the dog stuck his nose in after her. Suki lashed out with a claw. The dog yelped and backed away. Suki cowered under the bush, her heart thundering.

It was a long time before she was brave enough to look out. It was still snowing heavily. Suki's stomach growled hungrily. She was cold and tired and wanted to be back in the cosy boot room. But which way was back? Whichever way she turned, the landscape was the same. The wind ruffled Suki's fur the wrong way and blew snow in her face. Blinking it away, she took a hesitant step forward. More snow whirled in her face, making her sneeze. Her whiskers twitched in discomfort. Maybe she should go in the other direction?

Suki turned round, but that was even worse. The wind and snow pushed her forward, making her stumble into a snow drift. It was icy cold! Suki changed direction again. If only Katie was here. She'd make things right.

'Meow!' called Suki, hoping that Katie would hear her.

The wind snatched up her cries and threw them back at her. It was too cold to stand around waiting for help. Full of determination, Suki set out to find her way back home.

The weather was turning bad, but the mayor was confident that the Ice Extravaganza would go ahead.

'We've only ever cancelled it once and that was due to a blizzard,' he said. After he and his wife had left there was just time for a quick tea before setting off.

Katie wanted to go and see Suki first but the queen wouldn't let her.

'Suki will be fine,' she said.

'But what about her tea?' asked Katie.

'I'll get one of the staff to feed her,' said the queen. 'Hurry up now! The king is opening the Extravaganza this year, so we mustn't be late.'

'I feel really bad about Suki,' Katie said to Becky as she zipped up her coat. She hadn't even been allowed to go to the boot room to collect her outdoor things. Two of the servants had brought everything to her.

'I feel bad too,' said Becky. 'Let's make it up to her tomorrow.'

'We're going home tomorrow,' Katie reminded her.

Katie left the chalet with a heavy feeling in her stomach. But the feeling began to lessen as the royal car approached the town. The snow-covered buildings were sparkling in the glow of multicoloured lights. There was a whole village of stalls with colourful awnings, and the air was rich with the smell of hog roast and hot chocolate. A huge brass band played a welcome to the royal family as they gathered on the small stage overlooking the ice rink.

When the king declared the Extravaganza open, everyone cheered and waved tiny paper flags. Katie was swept up in the excitement and soon she was cheering too as the first competitors took to the ice for the speed-skating championships. After the races, Katie and Becky collected a map that showed the position of all the entries for the

snow sculpture competition. The girls were thrilled to see their own igloo marked on the map with a cross. It was great fun following the trail and stopping to admire each of the snow figures.

'This is my
favourite,' said Katie
as she stood in front
of a huge snow
palace. 'It's lit inside
with candles. I don't
know how they stop
it from melting!'

'I like the snow pony best,' Becky said. 'It's
big enough to ride.'

'That is
amazing too,'
Katie agreed.
The snow palace
came first and the
snow pony took
joint second place
with a snow dragon.

'At least the judges recognised our entry was an igloo,' said Katie, smiling as she pinned the blue rosette they'd won onto Becky's jacket.

'It's your rosette too,' said Becky, trying to stop her.

'We'll share it,' said Katie. 'You can wear it first.'

As the evening grew later, it began to snow even more. The wind grew stronger,

flinging the snow into drifts. By nine-thirty, the organisers decided to end early with the firework display.

'If they leave it any later, it will be too windy,' said the king.

Katie and Becky held hands while the fireworks whizzed and banged in the sky above them.

'Oooh!' gasped Katie as a rocket exploded in a shower of pink and purple stars.

The display ended with a hundred rockets raining red, gold and blue stars down from the sky together. As the last gold star dissolved, a hush fell over the town. Then all at once everyone clapped.

'That was amazing,' whispered Katie.

Linking arms, Katie and Becky walked back to the royal car. Alfie was so tired he fell asleep on the short ride home and had to be carried up to his room.

'Bed!' yawned Becky sleepily.

'In a minute,' said Katie, pulling off her boots. There was something she had to do first, if only she could remember what it was.

'Suki!' she cried, standing up straight. How could she have forgotten!

Guiltily, she ran along to the boot room to

say goodnight. She tiptoed into the room letting the light spill in from the hall in case the kitten was sleeping.

Suki's bed was empty.

Katie's heart thumped loudly.

'Suki!' she called, spinning round.

'She's got to be here somewhere,' said Becky, snapping on the light.

'She's not!' Katie's voice rose.

'She *must* be,' said Becky.

But the boot room was empty. Suki had gone.

Chapter 7

Lost in the Snow

Katie and Becky searched the whole of the royal chalet, pulling cushions off chairs and looking under all the beds, in case Suki was hiding somewhere. When they didn't find her, Mrs Philips went outside and walked around the gardens with a torch. It was very windy and she came back covered in snow.

'Nothing,' she said with a frown, brushing snowflakes from her hair.

'She's definitely not in here, so she must be outside somewhere,' said Katie, anxiously. 'We have to go and look for her or she'll freeze.'

The king and queen were getting ready for bed and were very surprised when Katie burst into their room. Quickly, she explained about Suki and asked if she and Becky could go and look for her.

'Not now!' exclaimed the queen. 'I'm sorry, Katie, but it's far too dark and stormy to go outside.'

'That's exactly why we have to go!' said Katie, desperately. 'Suki won't last the night if she's left out in this.'

The king sighed heavily. 'You and those

kittens! Well, you definitely can't go out on your own. Go and wait downstairs while I get dressed and I'll come with you.'

'Thank you, Dad!' squealed Katie, giving him a hug.

In the end, the queen and Mrs Philips joined the search party too. Mrs Philips made Katie and Becky put on gloves and scarves and handed out torches. It was very dark outside. Clouds scudded across the sky and snowflakes whirled in the wind. Walking was an effort. Katie's boots sank deep in the snow and the wind pushed her back. Holding hands with Becky, she struggled on, sweeping the snow with her torch beam.

The royal search party looked in the gardens, just in case Suki had come back, or Mrs Philips had missed her the first time.

Katie shone her torch up trees and under bushes. There was no sign of any animals at all. It seemed that everything had taken cover for the night.

Once they'd searched the grounds, they continued on through the main gates. It looked so different at night and, with the snow falling thickly, Katie almost didn't recognise

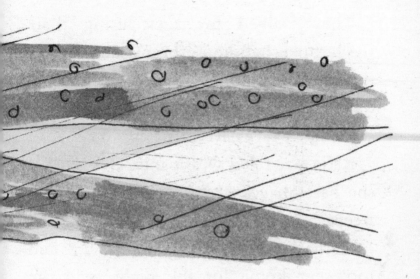

her igloo when she passed it. It had a fresh layer of snow covering it, making it look like a huge upside-down pudding. Snowflakes stung Katie's face and she sank deeper into her ski jacket, grateful for its warmth.

'Suki must be freezing,' she whispered to Becky. The girls looked at each other with tears in their eyes.

They walked for ages, using their torches like lighthouse beams until at last the king stopped.

'It's time to go back,' he said firmly. 'I'm sure Suki won't have come this far.'

Katie was filled with panic. 'But what if she has? She can't stay out in this. She'll freeze.'

'Perhaps someone else found her and took her home for the night,' said the queen reassuringly.

But what if they hadn't? Katie fell quiet. The thought that Suki might be lost in the snow at night made her breathless with fear. They walked on, past the igloo, its entrance tunnel now almost blocked by a snowdrift.

Suddenly Katie had an idea. There was

one place they hadn't looked. And the king had said that cats liked familiar places . . . She stopped walking.

'Keep going, darling,' said the queen. 'You'll freeze if you stand still.'

'Wait!' said Katie, turning back to the igloo.

She tried to run, but it was impossible. She shuffled back to the igloo and bent down to

shovel the snow away from the entrance with her hands. Even with her ski gloves on, her fingers were soon stinging with the cold. Becky joined her and when they had cleared enough snow away, Katie crawled into the igloo, shining her torch ahead of her. Becky followed close behind. It was spooky in the dark and full of shadows. What was that on the floor? Heart thumping, Katie aimed her torch at the strange-looking bundle. Suddenly it moved and a pair of large blue eyes shone back at her.

'Suki!'

The little kitten was curled up in the scarf nest that Katie had made the day they took Suki to the igloo. Her fur was grubby and matted together in spiky clumps and she was shivering. She tried to stand, but her legs were too wobbly and she sank back onto the scarf.

Katie pounced. Unzipping her coat, she gently tucked Suki inside, carefully zipping it back up so that only Suki's head was sticking out.

'Oh, Suki,' she said, fighting back her tears. 'I thought I'd lost you forever.'

'Purrrip!' croaked Suki, nudging Katie's hand.

'That's amazing! How did you know she was here?' asked Becky, leaning forward to stroke Suki's head.

'I don't know. It was just a feeling.'

'Thank goodness for feelings,' said Becky happily.

'Look who we found!' called Katie as they crawled out of the igloo.

'Darling, that's wonderful. Is she all right?' asked the queen.

'She's wet and very cold,' said Katie.

'We'd better get her indoors quickly,' said the king. 'Shall I carry her?'

'No, thanks. I can manage.' Katie wasn't letting Suki out of her sight again.

'Hot chocolate all round,' said Mrs Philips

leading the way to the kitchen when they reached the royal chalet.

Mrs Philips put a pan of milk on the hob to warm, then she fetched a towel. Katie and Becky sat side by side

on the floor and gently rubbed Suki dry. It was ages before she stopped shivering.

'Is she going to be all right?' asked Katie, worried.

'Try giving her this warm milk – that should help,' said Mrs Philips.

At first, Suki didn't seem to have the

energy to take the milk. Katie dipped her finger in it and put it by the kitten's mouth. Suki sniffed at it halfheartedly. Katie wiggled her finger. Suki's whiskers twitched, then she stuck out her tongue and licked Katie's finger. Once she had the taste of the milk, she licked faster. When the milk had gone, Katie gave her some more. Suki lapped it eagerly, so Katie offered her the saucer. Crouching low, Suki drank all the milk and licked the saucer clean.

'She's starving. Shall I give her some cat food?' Katie asked.

'A little,' said Mrs Philips. 'Be careful not to overfill her when she's had such a shock.'

Becky stood up. 'I'll get the cat food,' she offered.

Katie didn't want to leave Suki, but that wasn't fair on Becky.

'I'll do it. You can hold Suki until I get back,' she said, generously.

'Are you sure? Thanks,' said Becky, beaming.

Katie dished up half a portion of food. Suki devoured it hungrily while Katie and Becky sipped hot chocolate. Suki finished eating just as the kitchen cuckoo clock began to sing the hour.

'Goodness!' exclaimed the queen, looking up in surprise as the wooden bird popped in and out of its clock house. 'It's midnight! Time for bed, everyone. Put Suki back in the boot room. It's lovely and warm in there.'

Katie gave Suki a cuddle. She could hear the kitten's heart gently beating next to her own. After the fright she'd had, she couldn't bear to let Suki be alone.

'Can I have her in my room? Please?'

The queen sighed. 'Just for tonight then,' she said with a smile.

'Thanks, Mum, you're brilliant!' Katie hugged the queen carefully, so as not to crush Suki.

'And as for you,' Katie told the kitten, as she and Becky went upstairs. 'We're going home tomorrow. I'm not letting you out of my sight again until we're back at Starlight Towers.'

'Meow,' Suki purred sleepily.

Home! She could hardly wait.

Princess Katie's Kittens

Win a kitten charm bracelet!

To enter this competition, help Princess Katie
unscramble the name of Poppy's favourite toy:

☆ **M S U O E** ☆

We will put all the correct entries into a draw
and select one lucky winner!
Go online to send us your answer at

PrincessKatiesKittens.co.uk

or send your entry on a postcard to:
Princess Katie's Kittens Competition,
Piccadilly Press, 5 Castle Road, London, NW1 8PR.
Don't forget to include your name and address.

☆ Good luck! ☆

Competition closes 31st December 2012

Search with Suki

Help Suki find everyone who lives at Starlight Palace in the grid opposite, then write down all the spare letters to reveal a message about what Suki was looking for first!

Katie   Queen   Bella   Pebbles

Alfie   Becky   Poppy   Misty

King   Pixie   Tilly

The secret message
from Suki is:

_ __ _____

___ _ _____

Princess Katie's Kittens

T	I	L	L	Y	I	P	Y	A
Q	M	P	I	X	I	E	P	B
L	U	K	I	N	G	B	P	E
B	O	E	O	K	A	B	O	L
E	I	I	E	N	L	L	P	L
C	G	T	F	N	F	E	O	A
K	R	A	A	M	I	S	T	Y
Y	T	K	I	A	E	R	A	!

Find more fun kitten activities
at princesskatieskittens.co.uk

Pixie
at the Palace

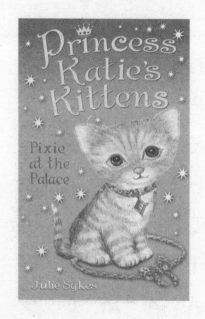

One of the newly found kittens has gone missing in the woods. Can Princess Katie and her best friend Becky find Pixie and bring him safely back to Starlight Palace?

Bella
at the Ball

Princess Katie is busy preparing for the queen's magnificent birthday ball, but Bella is busy getting into mischief! Katie and Becky must hurry to put things right, or the whole ball will be ruined!

Poppy
and the Prince

Poppy tries to make friends with Prince
Edward, who thinks cats are silly – but
when the prince gets lost in the palace
maze, it's Poppy who saves the day!

Princess Katie's Kittens

PrincessKatiesKittens.co.uk

Secret facts about the kittens
Kitten puzzles and activities
Princess Katie's top kitten care tips
Competitions
Book news and more!